The Cursed Paw of Ambition

The Cursed Paw of Ambition

Matthew Petchinsky

The Cursed Paw of Ambition
By: Matthew Petchinsky

Disclaimer:

This story is a unique variation inspired by the classic tale *The Monkey's Paw* by W.W. Jacobs, a story that has long fascinated audiences with its exploration of wishes and their unintended consequences. While this work pays homage to the original in spirit, it is not a replication of W.W. Jacobs' narrative, characters, or specific plot developments. Instead, it serves as a new creation that expands upon the core theme of wish fulfillment and its often dark repercussions, introducing fresh elements, characters, and unique twists.

The themes in this story delve into the broader implications of desire, ambition, and the unforeseen outcomes that accompany decisions born of longing and desperation. This work incorporates modern storytelling techniques, relatable motives, and scenarios distinct from the source material, offering readers a different perspective on the concept of "be careful what you wish for."

This story does not seek to copy or replace *The Monkey's Paw*; rather, it draws inspiration from its cautionary premise and builds an original plot enriched with new conflicts and unique consequences for each wish. Any resemblance to the original tale is solely thematic and is intended as a respectful nod to the timeless narrative that inspired countless writers and readers.

Readers should understand that while the core concept may echo a familiar moral lesson, the events, characters, and outcomes presented here are fully original and have been crafted to create an experience that stands independently as a modern story in its own right. This piece aims to spark curiosity, reflection, and suspense without diminishing the legacy of the work that inspired it.

Chapter 1: The Witch's Warning

The wind howled through the darkened streets, sending shivers through the narrow alleyways and rattling the old wooden signs that swung above shops long forgotten. Rain slashed against the cobblestones, turning them slick and treacherous. Elliott Barker, a reserved man with sharp, observant eyes and a slight frame draped in a worn trench coat, pulled his collar tighter around his neck and squinted through the sheets of rain. His gaze landed on a faintly glowing sign that read *Morgana's Mystical Emporium*, the letters curling like smoke.

"Never noticed that before," Elliott muttered, more to himself than the cold wind that responded with a mournful moan. Curiosity piqued, he stepped forward, pushing open the heavy oak door. A bell chimed with an eerie, hollow sound, announcing his presence.

The inside of the shop was a labyrinth of ancient books, jars filled with unrecognizable substances, and artifacts that seemed to whisper secrets if one listened closely enough. The air was thick with the scent of incense—clove and something more bitter. Shadows danced across the walls as candles flickered, their flames casting a dim glow that barely pushed back the darkness.

"Welcome," a voice rasped, startling Elliott. He turned sharply and found himself face-to-face with an old woman, her dark eyes sharp as a raven's, set deep into a lined face framed by silver hair that spilled over her shoulders like a storm cloud. She was draped in layers of flowing robes, adorned with beads and symbols that hinted at their mystical origins.

"I didn't mean to intrude," Elliott said, his voice more confident than he felt.

"Few come here without reason," the old woman replied, her lips curling into a smile that was anything but warm. "I am Morgana, keeper of this place. What brings you to my door on such a night?"

Elliott shifted uneasily, glancing around. His eyes fell on a glass box perched on a velvet pedestal, half-hidden behind jars of dried herbs and scrolls. Inside, a shriveled, mummified monkey's paw stood upright, its three fingers raised in a silent, eerie gesture.

Morgana followed his gaze and let out a low chuckle that sent a shiver down Elliott's spine. "Ah, the monkey's paw. A curious item, that one. Powerful, dangerous."

Elliott stepped closer, his eyes narrowing as he studied the relic. It was grotesque, the fur still clinging to its gnarled surface in patches, and the fingers stiff with a mockery of life. "What is it?" he asked, though a part of him already knew.

"It is a talisman of old," Morgana said, moving with surprising grace to stand beside him. "It grants its owner three wishes, each one fulfilled with a price."

"A price?" Elliott echoed, a skeptical smile tugging at the corners of his mouth.

The witch's eyes locked onto his with an intensity that made him shift his weight. "Be careful what you wish for, young man. The paw twists desire into consequence. Greed, ambition, even love—each comes with a cost." She reached out with bony fingers and tapped on the glass. "Those who wield it think themselves clever. But fate, my dear, has a wicked sense of humor."

Elliott's gaze returned to the paw, a strange thrill coursing through him. He had spent years toiling away in a mundane job, each day blending into the next. The idea of bending fate, of finally having the power to change his life, was irresistible.

"How much?" he asked, his voice firmer now.

Morgana's smile faltered, replaced by a look of sadness, as if she could see the path he was about to take. "You cannot buy this thinking it is a trinket. It is a chain, and its weight will find you."

"How much?" Elliott repeated, more forcefully this time.

The witch sighed, her eyes darkening with resignation. "One hundred and fifty pounds," she said finally. The amount was steep, more than he'd usually consider for a whim, but something in the air—perhaps the flicker of destiny itself—pushed him forward.

He reached into his coat, pulled out his wallet, and counted out the bills. Morgana accepted them with a frown, fingers lingering over his hand as if she wanted to pull it back.

"Remember," she said, her voice barely above a whisper, "it grants three wishes. Use them wisely, or not at all."

Elliott nodded absently, already lost in the what-ifs swirling in his mind. He took the glass box in both hands, the weight of it far heavier than he expected, and left without another word. The bell chimed behind him, its hollow echo mixing with the growing storm outside.

"Good luck," Morgana called after him, though her tone suggested that luck had little to do with it.

As the door swung shut, the shop fell into a silence broken only by the crackle of a single candle. Morgana gazed at the empty spot where the paw had stood, her eyes distant, as though seeing events unfold far beyond the confines of her shop.

"May you find what you seek," she murmured, "and survive what follows."

Chapter 2: The First Wish – Fortune's Cost

Elliott stood in the dim glow of his apartment, the silence broken only by the soft hum of the refrigerator and the occasional patter of rain against the window. The monkey's paw sat on his coffee table, grotesque and silent. He had placed it carefully, as if it were an idol of some ancient deity, one that might wake if disturbed. The three fingers, dry and shriveled, pointed skyward, an eerie mockery of a salute.

He sank into his worn armchair, eyes fixed on the paw as if it might move on its own. A rush of thoughts swirled in his mind—doubt, anticipation, the echo of Morgana's warning. *Each wish comes with a price.* The old witch's voice seemed to hiss in the corners of the room, making the hair on his arms stand up.

"Come on, Elliott, it's just a relic," he muttered to himself, though the words rang hollow. He rubbed his hands together, the cold from the paw's presence creeping into his bones. After a deep breath, he spoke aloud, each word laden with a nervous quiver.

"I wish to win the lottery. Enough to be set for life."

A moment passed where nothing happened. The room, the paw, even the air itself, seemed to hold its breath. Then, slowly and with a quiet creak that sounded almost like a sigh, the middle finger of the paw curled downward. A chill coursed through Elliott's spine, leaving him momentarily paralyzed. He shook it off, laughing nervously.

"That's it? No fireworks? No ominous thunder?" He stood, trying to convince himself that it was nothing more than an elaborate prank.

The rain continued its rhythm outside, indifferent to his skepticism. The paw remained still, its two fingers raised in a silent warning.

Morning light filtered through the blinds, casting thin, pale stripes across the living room. Elliott woke up on the couch, the weight of the previous night's events still pressing on his chest. He glanced at the paw, now just an unmoving relic on the table. "What was I expecting?" he murmured, rubbing his temples.

A loud vibration startled him. His phone buzzed on the table, screen lit up with the name *Local News Alert*.

"Winner Announced: The $50 Million Lottery Goes to Elliott Barker of Hillside."

His heart stopped, then started again with a racing fury. "No way." He tapped the notification, and there it was: his name printed in bold, confirming the unbelievable. He stumbled to his feet, pacing the room as adrenaline surged through him.

A knock at the door made him jump. Peeking through the peephole, he saw Mrs. Lowry, the elderly neighbor who often checked in on him with unsolicited advice and casseroles. He took a deep breath and opened the door, trying to hide his elation.

"Elliott, did you hear?" she said, eyes wide, clutching her robe tight against her chest. "You've won! It's on the news! $50 million! I almost fainted when I saw it."

"I, uh, yeah, I did," he stammered, a grin breaking through despite himself. "It's surreal."

"Surreal, indeed!" Mrs. Lowry laughed, patting his arm with a shaky hand. "You're a lucky man. You take care now, and don't let them big city types come and swindle you out of it."

"I won't, Mrs. Lowry. Thanks for checking in," he said, gently closing the door. The room felt smaller, the air electric with the knowledge that everything was about to change.

Elliott spent the rest of the day in a whirlwind of phone calls from the lottery commission, bank representatives, and even a few reporters. By the afternoon, he sat back, exhausted but euphoric. *I really did it. I beat the odds.*

But then, his phone buzzed with a new notification: an email from *Jasper & Co. Publishing*—his employer.

Subject: *Notice of Termination Due to Budget Cuts.*

He read the subject line again, the letters blurring as disbelief set in. Opening the email, the reality hit like a punch to the gut:

Dear Mr. Barker,

Due to unforeseen financial constraints, the company has made the difficult decision to reduce staff. Your role will be terminated effective immediately. We appreciate your contributions and wish you the best in your future endeavors.

Sincerely,

Human Resources

He stared at the screen, numbness seeping into his bones. "Unforeseen? How convenient," he whispered, the irony twisting in his chest like a knife. Here he was, $50 million richer, yet stripped of his job, his security. The laughter that bubbled up was bitter, almost hysterical.

The paw sat motionless on the table, two fingers raised, as if mocking him.

"So that's the game," Elliott said aloud, eyes narrowing at the cursed relic. "I win, but I lose. Let's see how far this goes."

The room darkened as the rainclouds thickened outside. The wind picked up, howling through the gaps in the window frames, carrying a whisper that sounded too much like Morgana's warning: *Each comes with a price.*

Chapter 3: Fame's Dark Side

Elliott sat at his mahogany desk, the monkey's paw lying just beyond his fingertips. The silence of the room felt heavy, interrupted only by the steady tick of the clock on the wall. The initial excitement from his lottery win had begun to wane, replaced by a gnawing sense of restlessness. Wealth, he realized, was not enough. He wanted recognition, not just for a stroke of luck but for something he created.

He glanced at the paw, eyes narrowing. It seemed to be watching him, daring him to take another step down the path he had chosen. With a shaky breath, Elliott closed his eyes and voiced his wish.

"I wish to become a world-famous author, known for my books and stories."

A crack echoed through the room as the second finger of the paw curled downward, sharper and more pronounced than before. The sound reverberated in his chest, leaving behind a chill that refused to dissipate. He pushed back his chair, suddenly feeling suffocated in his own home.

"Well, let's see what happens now," he muttered, attempting to shake off the foreboding feeling.

The next morning, Elliott woke to the unmistakable *ping* of his phone's notifications. The screen was a mess of alerts, emails, and messages. His brow furrowed as he unlocked the device and scrolled through the barrage of headlines:

"Unknown Author's Book Takes Literary World by Storm!"

"Meet Elliott Barker: The Overnight Sensation You Need to Know."

His fingers trembled as he opened his inbox. There were thousands of emails, from literary agents to publishing houses and journalists clamoring for interviews.

"What... How?" he whispered, heart thudding in his chest.

A knock on the door jolted him out of his thoughts. He peered through the peephole to find two men with cameras slung around their necks, already snapping photos and shouting his name.

"Mr. Barker! Elliott, can we get a few words for the press?" one of them called, his voice muffled by the door.

Elliott backed away, the walls of his small apartment seeming to close in around him. The phone buzzed again, vibrating with the energy of a life he hadn't been ready for. His initial exhilaration at the wish's fulfillment soured into anxiety as he realized the implications.

A sudden bang at the window made him jump. He turned to see a teenage girl pressing her face against the glass, eyes wide with excitement. "Elliott! Oh my god, it's really you!" she screamed, her voice barely audible through the barrier.

Elliott's stomach churned. He closed the curtains, blocking out her eager face but not the thrum of panic coursing through him. The once comforting walls of his home now felt like a cage, and outside, the world seemed to be clawing at him, desperate to get in.

Days turned into weeks, and the relentless spotlight only intensified. Elliott's stories topped bestseller lists, and AI-generated novels bearing his name were consumed by millions. Each new release was met with fanfare, but the cost of his newfound fame loomed large. His phone rang constantly, friends from the past suddenly resurfacing, claiming connections they never had. He barely slept, haunted by the ringing phone and the buzz of reporters camping outside.

A sharp rap on his door one evening made him jump. He peeked through the window, heart sinking when he saw a man wearing a badge that read *Freelance Journalist*. Elliott ignored it, pressing his back to the wall and sliding down to the floor.

Suddenly, a letter slipped through the mail slot and landed on the rug. It was pink, scrawled with red ink in looping letters.

"I love you, Elliott. I know where you live. We're meant to be together."

He crumpled the note with shaking hands and stood abruptly, pacing the room. The fame that had seemed so glamorous in his wish now felt like a curse.

A frantic knock on the door followed, accompanied by a man's voice. "Elliott! Come on, just one interview! Your fans are dying for a personal look into your life!"

"No," Elliott whispered, running his fingers through his hair. "No, this is too much."

The paw lay on the table, now with two fingers curled, the final one standing ominously upright. He glared at it, feeling anger bubble up in his chest.

"You did this," he said, voice breaking. "This is your doing."

The night deepened, bringing with it shadows that crept across the room like specters. Outside, cameras flashed periodically as the paparazzi caught glimpses through the thin curtains. The once comforting drone of the city now felt like a chant of strangers' voices, relentless and inescapable.

Elliott grabbed the paw, the weight of it colder than he remembered. He needed a way out, a solution that wouldn't backfire. But the paw, with its sinister promise, seemed to whisper that every wish came with a twist, and he wasn't sure he could endure one more.

He dropped the relic back on the table, the sound echoing through the room. The paw remained still, its single finger raised, a silent promise that there was one more wish—and one more consequence—waiting for him.

Chapter 4: The Return of Whiskers

Elliott sat hunched on the edge of his bed, the muffled voices of reporters and fans clamoring outside his window like a chorus of relentless specters. He hadn't left his apartment in days, the weight of fame pressing on him like a lead blanket. The once-exhilarating glow of success had turned toxic, seeping into his every thought and movement.

His eyes fell on the monkey's paw lying on the table, now with only one finger raised. It seemed to taunt him, daring him to use his final wish. He wiped at the tears that pricked his eyes, exhaustion and loneliness gnawing at him. In the flurry of fame and endless attention, he had no one to turn to, no one he trusted. But then, his mind wandered back to the warm, comforting presence of Whiskers, his cat who had passed away years ago. The thought filled him with a longing so deep it ached in his chest.

He stood up, walked over to the paw, and picked it up with trembling hands. "All I ever wanted was a bit of happiness," he whispered. "Is that too much to ask?"

The room seemed to listen, the faint buzz of the city outside dulling as he took a shaky breath.

"I wish for Whiskers to come back to me," he said, each word dropping like a stone in the silence.

The paw's final finger curled down with an audible snap, and a chill swept through the room. It felt as though the temperature had plummeted, frost skimming the edges of the windowpane. Elliott shuddered and set the paw down, its weight now feeling unbearably heavy in his hand. The silence that followed was deep and unnatural, stretching on until every creak of the floorboards made him flinch.

Night fell, swallowing the city in its obsidian cloak. The voices outside had faded, replaced by the occasional flash of a camera and murmured conversations. Elliott sat in his armchair, the room dark but for the soft glow of a single lamp. His head drooped as exhaustion pulled at him.

Then he heard it: the faintest *scritch* of paws against wood, followed by a low, familiar purr. His eyes snapped open, heart pounding.

"Whiskers?" he called, voice barely above a whisper.

From the shadows near the hallway, a small shape slinked into view. At first, Elliott's breath caught in disbelief. The cat, its gray fur just as he remembered, stared at him with wide, green eyes. It blinked slowly, and a shiver of joy ran through him.

"Oh, Whiskers!" He fell to his knees, arms outstretched. The cat approached cautiously, the purr growing louder as it rubbed against his arm. Elliott's eyes flooded with tears, and he let out a sound that was half-laughter, half-sob.

"I missed you so much," he said, pressing his cheek against the soft fur. Whiskers mewed in response, the sound comforting and familiar.

But as the night wore on, Elliott noticed small, unsettling details. Whiskers' eyes glimmered with an unnatural light, and his movements, though fluid, were sharp and precise, almost mechanical. The cat would freeze mid-stride, ears flicking as though listening to sounds only he could hear, before continuing with an eerie grace.

Later, as Elliott lay in bed with Whiskers curled at his feet, a sudden noise jolted him awake. It was a low, guttural growl. He sat up slowly and saw Whiskers, fur bristled and eyes fixed on the dark corner of the room. The cat's pupils were narrow slits, glinting like emerald blades.

"What is it, buddy?" Elliott whispered, though fear coiled in his gut.

Whiskers hissed, a long, feral sound that seemed to resonate deep in Elliott's chest. The cat sprang from the bed and landed on the floor with a thud, slinking toward the corner, tail lashing violently. Elliott reached for his phone, its screen casting a small pool of light that did little to chase away the shadows.

"Whiskers, calm down," he said, trying to steady his voice. But as he reached out, Whiskers turned to him with a gaze that was anything but familiar. The green eyes glowed, and a low, rumbling purr filled the room—a sound that felt more like a warning than a comfort.

The cat leaped onto the bed, claws extended, and raked them across the blanket with such force that it shredded. Elliott gasped and pulled back, nearly tumbling off the bed.

"Stop!" he shouted, the command breaking the strange trance in the air.

Whiskers paused, head cocked as if considering the order. The unnatural gleam faded from his eyes, and he meowed softly, almost apologetically, before jumping down and padding out of the room.

Elliott sat there, heart hammering against his ribs, skin prickling with cold sweat. He cast a glance at the table, where the monkey's paw lay, its fingers now all curled into a tight, lifeless fist.

He realized with a sinking heart that his wish had been granted, but in the way all wishes made to the paw were fulfilled—twisted, corrupted, and crawling with consequences.

From the hallway, the sound of claws tapping against the floor grew fainter as Whiskers disappeared into the shadows, leaving Elliott wide awake and steeped in dread.

Chapter 5: The Unraveling

Elliott sat at his kitchen table, the early morning light casting long, thin shadows across the room. His hands wrapped tightly around a mug of coffee that had gone cold, eyes bloodshot from another sleepless night. Whiskers sat in the corner, tail flicking back and forth, eyes fixed on a spot just above Elliott's head. The cat's stare had become an almost permanent fixture of Elliott's day, an unspoken challenge that sent shivers down his spine.

"Whiskers," he muttered, more to himself than to the animal. "What are you looking at?"

The cat's eyes, glowing with that unnatural intensity, didn't waver. Instead, he let out a low, menacing growl that seemed to vibrate through the floor. Elliott's fingers tightened on the mug, the ceramic biting into his skin.

"I can't do this," he whispered, a tremor in his voice.

The phone on the table buzzed with a new notification, making him jump and spill a line of coffee down the front of his shirt. Cursing under his breath, he grabbed a napkin, eyes darting to Whiskers, who was now watching him with an expression that could only be described as knowing.

This is insane, Elliott thought, pressing the damp cloth to his chest. He had ignored the signs for days now—Whiskers pacing back and forth as if patrolling an invisible perimeter, his sudden hisses at corners of the room that seemed empty, and the inexplicable crashes in the night that left broken glass and toppled shelves in their wake.

That night, as darkness settled in, Elliott lay on his bed, staring at the ceiling. The familiar glow of streetlights seeped through the blinds, painting thin lines across the room. Whiskers was nowhere to be seen, which made Elliott's skin prickle. The silence was oppressive, broken only by the occasional creak of the floorboards, the house groaning like an old ship at sea.

A faint *thud* echoed from the hallway, and Elliott's body stiffened. He listened, heart pounding in his ears. The sound came again, followed by the quiet tap-tap of claws on the hardwood floor. His breath quickened as the noise approached, stopping just outside the bedroom door.

"Whiskers?" His voice cracked.

A low, rumbling purr was the only response. Elliott sat up slowly, eyes locked on the door, the weak light from the hallway seeping in through the small gap at the bottom. Suddenly, shadows shifted, and the cat's silhouette appeared. But there was something wrong. Whiskers' body was stiff, eyes reflecting an unnatural green light that cast tiny points of fire onto the floor.

The cat let out a sound—half-purr, half-growl—that sent Elliott scrambling back against the headboard. Whiskers slinked into the room, moving like liquid, eyes never breaking contact.

"Stay back," Elliott said, holding out his hand as if to ward off a wild animal. The cat paused, head cocked as if considering his plea. Then, with a sudden burst of motion, Whiskers leapt onto the bed, claws raking the blanket and barely missing Elliott's leg.

"Damn it!" Elliott shouted, heart slamming in his chest. He kicked out reflexively, sending Whiskers skittering off the bed with a hiss. The cat's eyes narrowed, and for a moment, Elliott swore he saw something human in them—anger, calculation.

The room felt colder, the shadows darker. He glanced at the monkey's paw on the nightstand, its fingers still curled tight. A wave of nausea rolled through him as the realization struck him again: this was no ordinary cat anymore, and this was no simple wish. It was a curse, one he had willingly invoked.

Over the next few days, Elliott tried to ignore the mounting evidence of his mistake. He avoided Whiskers, keeping to the kitchen or the living room, leaving food and water in their bowls as a peace offering. But the cat's behavior grew more erratic. He knocked over vases, shredded the couch cushions, and hissed at unseen things that seemed to fill the room with a palpable tension.

"Why won't you just go away?" Elliott whispered one afternoon, head in his hands as he sat at the table. The cat had taken to pacing the perimeter of the room, eyes flicking to Elliott with each pass.

A knock at the window startled him, and he looked up to see a face peering in—a young reporter, notebook in hand, eyes wide with determination.

"Mr. Barker! Just a few questions, please!" she shouted, rapping on the glass. Elliott stood abruptly, crossing the room in two quick strides.

"Leave me alone!" he shouted back, pounding his fist against the window. The reporter's eyes widened before she scurried off, the sound of her hurried footsteps fading down the street.

"Great, now even more attention," he muttered, turning back to find Whiskers sitting in the doorway, tail swishing lazily. The cat's eyes glowed like embers, and a low, rumbling purr filled the room, vibrating through Elliott's bones. It felt more like a growl, a warning.

The phone buzzed with another notification, the screen lighting up with a headline: *"Author Elliott Barker's Sudden Fame Draws Attention—Fans Camp Outside Home."*

Elliott's fingers twitched, a mix of frustration and panic coursing through him. He knew he was losing control—control of his life, his mind, and whatever this twisted thing Whiskers had become. The walls of the apartment seemed to close in, suffocating him with the weight of his choices.

He backed into the living room, eyes darting between Whiskers and the locked front door, as if calculating the possibility of escape. But as the cat's tail flicked and his purr deepened, Elliott realized that this was no longer just about the fame or the wealth or the wishes that had come true. It was about survival. And Whiskers, his once-beloved companion, had become something else entirely—a living embodiment of the price he'd paid.

A price he knew he'd never escape.

Chapter 6: The Final Consequence

The oppressive silence of the apartment was punctuated only by the rhythmic tick of the clock and the distant hum of traffic. The night outside was as dark as ink, the kind that seemed to swallow the world whole. Elliott lay in a restless sleep, sheets twisted around his legs and sweat dampening his brow. He dreamed of shadows moving across his walls, eyes watching him, claws scraping the floor.

A sudden weight pressed down on his chest, heavy and suffocating. His eyes flew open, breath hitching in his throat. Whiskers sat atop him, eyes like burning coals fixed on Elliott's wide, terrified gaze. The cat's fur bristled, and a guttural, otherworldly growl rumbled from deep within its small frame.

"Whiskers?" Elliott's voice was hoarse, barely more than a whisper. He couldn't move, couldn't think past the primal fear that clamped around his body like a vise.

The cat's eyes narrowed, glistening with a malicious light that sent shivers down Elliott's spine. Before he could react, Whiskers lunged, sharp claws slicing into the soft flesh of his cheek. Pain exploded across his face, hot and wet. Elliott gasped, instinctively trying to push the cat away, but Whiskers latched onto his arm, teeth sinking into the tender skin.

"Stop! Whiskers, stop!" Elliott cried, his voice breaking into a high-pitched wail as the cat's claws raked his chest. Blood seeped through his shirt, the metallic tang filling his nostrils as his vision blurred with tears and shock.

The room seemed to warp, the shadows lengthening, twisting in on themselves as if feeding off the violence. The cat's growls grew louder, more feral, echoing in Elliott's ears until they became indistinguishable from his own screams. His strength waned, the fight draining from him as the searing pain ebbed and was replaced by a numbing cold.

Whiskers' eyes were the last thing he saw before darkness engulfed him, burning like twin suns, full of ancient, vengeful knowledge.

Morning light seeped into the apartment, casting long golden beams that illuminated the chaos of the night before. Broken furniture, papers strewn across the floor, and dark smears of blood told a story of violence that the silence now refused to betray.

The sound of muffled voices and the crackle of a police radio broke the stillness as officers stepped into the living room, eyes wide with the realization that something terrible had occurred. Detective Harris, a seasoned man with tired eyes and a jaw set like granite, surveyed the scene.

"Jesus," one of the officers muttered, crossing himself as he looked down at Elliott's lifeless form. He was sprawled on the bed, eyes frozen open in a final, silent scream, his body marked with deep gashes.

Harris' gaze fell on the peculiar object near Elliott's outstretched hand: a mummified monkey's paw, its fingers curled tightly into a sinister fist. He leaned down, touching it with gloved fingers. The air seemed colder around it, and a shiver ran down his spine.

"No signs of forced entry," Harris said, almost to himself. "But this..." He trailed off, glancing at the other officers who exchanged puzzled looks. The scene defied explanation.

Across town, Morgana sat in her dimly lit shop, watching the news coverage on an old television set that flickered with static. The reporter's voice trembled as she recounted the strange and tragic death of Elliott Barker, the overnight literary sensation whose life had been marked by an inexplicable string of events.

"The authorities remain puzzled by the cause of death. While there were clear injuries, no evidence points to another person being involved. The only item of note found at the scene was an unusual artifact, identified as a monkey's paw."

Morgana's lips twitched, a shadow of a smile playing on her face as she leaned back in her chair, eyes glinting with a knowing sadness. She reached for her cup of tea, the steam curling around her fingers like ghostly tendrils.

"Ambition," she murmured, voice low and heavy with the weight of truth, "has always been a double-edged sword."

The screen flashed images of Elliott, taken in happier times, oblivious to the fate that would befall him. Morgana sighed, eyes drifting to the dark corners of her shop where other relics sat, waiting.

Outside, the rain began to fall, tapping against the window like an old, familiar refrain, and Morgana whispered a final word to the room. "And the price is always paid."

Appendices

Appendix A: Author's Note: An Analysis of the Consequences of Ambition and the Cautionary Themes Inspired by Classic Folklore

In crafting *The Cursed Paw of Ambition*, my aim was to delve deep into the timeless themes of desire, ambition, and the price that often accompanies them. These themes, interwoven with cautionary tales and folklore, resonate across cultures and generations. At its heart, this story explores how unchecked ambition can lead to consequences that, while not immediately apparent, are insidious and devastating.

The Allure and Price of Ambition

Ambition is a double-edged sword, a driving force that has the power to uplift or destroy. In Elliott Barker's story, we see ambition embodied in the choices he makes after acquiring the monkey's paw—a talisman known for granting wishes with twisted results. His journey from a humble, disillusioned man to a world-famous author reveals how desires, when fulfilled without consideration of consequence, come at a profound cost.

Elliott's first wish, born from a desire for wealth, highlights the human tendency to equate money with freedom and happiness. Winning the lottery brings him immediate joy, but the consequences are swift and cutting: unemployment and the realization that wealth alone cannot buy peace or purpose. This wish sets the stage for the overarching message of the story—that ambition driven solely by material or superficial gains is inherently flawed.

His second wish, to become a world-famous author, is rooted in the human craving for recognition and validation. This is a universal desire: the need to be seen, heard, and appreciated. However, fame is a complex and fickle master. As Elliott discovers, it brings with it a loss of privacy, the intrusion of relentless fans, and the suffocating pressure of public scrutiny. The second wish exposes the reader to the harsh reality that notoriety, while enticing, can strip away personal autonomy and peace of mind.

Folklore and the Cautionary Tale Tradition

The concept of wishes bearing unforeseen consequences is a motif that appears frequently in folklore and myth, spanning different cultures and times. Stories like W.W. Jacobs' *The Monkey's Paw*, which inspired this work, serve as warnings against tampering with fate. The paw itself is an emblem of temptation and hubris, offering power that is both coveted and feared.

In Elliott's final wish, we see the purest and most tragic form of longing: the desire to reclaim lost love and companionship. This wish, unlike the others, is not rooted in ambition for success or wealth but in an aching need for comfort. Yet, even this wish, seemingly innocent, is not spared from the paw's dark nature. The resurrection of Whiskers, Elliott's beloved cat, acts as a mirror to his desperation and the lengths to which he would go to alleviate his loneliness. The creature that returns is not the companion he remembered but a vessel of eerie intelligence and malevolent will. It symbolizes how desires that defy the natural order can disrupt the balance of life and death, bringing more pain than peace.

Ambition Versus Contentment

The broader question raised by *The Cursed Paw of Ambition* is one that echoes through countless cautionary tales: When is enough, enough? Elliott's relentless pursuit of more—more wealth, more recognition, more love—ultimately isolates him. This narrative reflects a critical aspect of human nature; the constant yearning for what lies beyond our reach can blind us to the value of what we already possess.

Ambition, when untethered from wisdom and humility, becomes self-destructive. Elliott's fate is sealed not by the wishes themselves but by his refusal to heed warnings and consider the potential costs of his actions. The story's climax, where Elliott realizes too late that his final wish was a grave mistake, serves as a powerful reminder of the consequences of ignoring the quiet voice of reason.

Lessons from the Folklore Tradition

The story draws on themes found in folklore, where characters often learn painful lessons about greed, power, and the consequences of playing god. From King Midas and his golden touch to Faust's bargain with Mephistopheles, these tales teach that the pursuit of unchecked ambition often leads to ruin. They are meant not just to entertain but to impart a moral, a reminder of the perils of human desire and the importance of moderation.

Morgana, the enigmatic witch who sells the paw to Elliott, represents the voice of forewarning, a guardian of the old knowledge that knows the true nature of the artifact. Her character embodies the wisdom of those who understand that not everything powerful is meant to be wielded. The final scene, where she reflects on Elliott's fate with the resigned observation, "Ambition has always been a double-edged sword," reinforces the story's message: that the pursuit of one's deepest desires, if done recklessly, will come at a cost.

Conclusion: The True Cost of Desire

In closing, *The Cursed Paw of Ambition* is more than a tale of supernatural horror; it is a narrative that invites reflection on the human condition. It asks us to consider the nature of our desires and the lengths we are willing to go to fulfill them. Elliott's story serves as a caution: that the most compelling desires, when granted without regard for consequence, can turn dreams into nightmares.

This story's message is clear: Ambition is necessary, even vital, for growth, but it must be balanced with foresight, humility, and a respect for the boundaries set by fate. The question it leaves readers with is simple but profound: If given the chance, would you make a wish knowing it could cost you everything?

Appendix B: Glossary: Descriptions of the Artifacts and Symbols Found in the Witch's Shop

Morgana's Mystical Emporium was a repository of arcane relics, each steeped in layers of history and supernatural lore. The items in her shop weren't just objects; they were fragments of stories, powerful echoes of forgotten eras, and bearers of mysteries that defied the ordinary. Below is an extensive glossary of some of the most intriguing artifacts and symbols found within the shadowed shelves and dusty corners of the shop.

1. The Monkey's Paw

- **Description**: A mummified, shriveled paw of a monkey, encased in a glass box. The paw has three raised fingers, each representing a wish that could be granted to its owner. The fur, though sparse and aged, clings in patches, and the bones are contorted, giving it an unsettling appearance.
- **Significance**: This relic is said to grant three wishes, but each comes with unforeseen consequences. The paw embodies the age-old cautionary tale of *be careful what you wish for*, serving as a reminder that power without wisdom often leads to ruin.
- **Origin**: Folklore suggests it was created by a sorcerer who wanted to teach people that fate governs life and should not be altered without repercussions.

2. The Seeing Orb of Thalassia

- **Description**: A deep blue, glass orb veined with thin streaks of silver that seem to shift when viewed at different angles. It rests on a pedestal carved with oceanic symbols like waves and fish scales.
- **Significance**: Known to show glimpses of possible futures or hidden truths when gazed into during a meditative state. However, the orb's visions are cryptic and prone to misinterpretation.

- **Origin**: Legend states it was gifted to a seer by the sea goddess Thalassia, who infused it with the power of the tides and the mysteries of the deep.

3. The Ouroboros Pendant

- **Description**: A bronze medallion featuring the ancient symbol of the snake devouring its own tail, set against an obsidian disk. The snake's eyes are small rubies, and the scales are etched with minute runes that are nearly imperceptible.
- **Significance**: The Ouroboros is an emblem of eternal cycles, life, and death, symbolizing the self-consuming, regenerating nature of existence. The pendant is said to offer insight into personal rebirth and transformation but can also trap the wearer in an endless loop of choices if misused.
- **Origin**: Found in the ruins of an ancient temple in Egypt, where priests believed it could invoke the cycle of life to predict death or birth.

4. The Witch's Athame

- **Description**: A ceremonial dagger with a hilt inlaid with onyx and a blade etched with symbols of the moon phases. It is kept in a sheath decorated with celestial patterns.
- **Significance**: Used for directing energy during rituals and spellcasting. The athame is not meant for physical cutting but is a spiritual tool of power. It represents willpower, direction, and the severing of negative ties.
- **Origin**: Believed to be crafted by a coven of witches during the medieval era, the athame was said to hold the combined essence of its creators, empowering it to channel spells of protection and binding.

5. The Book of Shadows

- **Description**: A heavy, leather-bound tome with pages yellowed by age and a cover engraved with an intricate tree motif whose branches morph into mystical symbols. The book has a faint scent of old parchment and sage.
- **Significance**: Contains spells, herbal remedies, and rituals compiled over generations of witches. The contents are said to adapt to its reader, revealing only what they are prepared to understand.
- **Origin**: Passed down from Morgana's lineage, it was once used by a high priestess who recorded her most potent spells within its pages. It's believed that a portion of her spirit resides in the book, offering cryptic guidance to those deemed worthy.

6. The Philosopher's Stone Fragment

- **Description**: A shard of deep crimson, translucent crystal that glows faintly when touched. It is kept in a small iron box lined with velvet and secured with intricate, silver-etched clasps.
- **Significance**: The philosopher's stone is fabled to grant eternal life and the ability to transmute base metals into gold. While this fragment lacks the power of the complete stone, it is said to have residual properties that boost vitality and intuition.
- **Origin**: Alchemists across Europe hunted for the legendary stone, and this piece is said to have been chipped from an original found by a medieval alchemist who perished before revealing its secrets.

7. The St. Elmo's Lantern

- **Description**: A brass lantern with panels made of stained glass that emit an ethereal, blue light when activated. The glass is etched with angelic sigils, and the handle is wrapped in worn leather.
- **Significance**: This lantern is said to harness the energy of St. Elmo's Fire, a natural phenomenon associated with electrical storms and regarded as a sign of divine presence or protection. When lit, it repels malevolent spirits and illuminates hidden paths.
- **Origin**: Reputed to have been blessed by sailors during treacherous sea voyages, the lantern protected its bearers from supernatural threats lurking beneath the waves.

8. The Whispering Jar

- **Description**: A small, earthenware jar painted with faded, spiral patterns. When held close, faint whispers can be heard emanating from within, as though the jar holds captured voices.
- **Significance**: The jar is said to contain the secrets or last words of those who have passed on. It can be used for guidance, but one must be wary, as the whispers can also sow confusion or deceit.
- **Origin**: Found in an old crypt in Eastern Europe, the jar was once used by shamans who believed it captured the knowledge of their ancestors.

9. The Phoenix Feather Quill

- **Description**: A vibrant, red-gold feather that shimmers as if aflame. It sits in an ink pot filled with ink that seems to glow faintly.
- **Significance**: Used for writing spells or recording prophecies, the feather is said to imbue words with the power of renewal and transformation. Any text written with it is said to endure for eternity and contain a spark of truth that reveals itself over time.
- **Origin**: Stories claim it was plucked from the tail of a living phoenix by a mystic who studied the art of eternal wisdom.

10. The Silver Bell of Lumen

- **Description**: A small, intricately carved silver bell that emits a soft, pure tone when rung. The bell is engraved with tiny runes that catch the light in mesmerizing patterns.
- **Significance**: Used in rituals to cleanse spaces of dark energy and ward off evil. Its chime is said to reach beyond the physical realm, calling upon benevolent spirits for protection or guidance.
- **Origin**: Forged in the ancient city of Lumen, where it was used in ceremonies to invoke divine favor and cast out malignant forces.

Each item in Morgana's shop holds power, history, and an allure that speaks to the deepest corners of human curiosity and fear. They are reminders that magic, like ambition, can be as treacherous as it is fascinating, carrying with it an echo of old lessons and the price one pays for tampering with the unknown.

Appendix C: Reflections on the Tale: A Breakdown of Elliott's Choices and Real-Life Lessons on Greed, Fame, and the Danger of Unchecked Desires

Elliott Barker's journey in *The Cursed Paw of Ambition* serves as an allegory for real-life struggles involving ambition, desire, and the pursuit of fulfillment. Each wish made by Elliott reflects choices that many face in the pursuit of wealth, recognition, and emotional comfort, showing how the consequences of those desires can unfold in unexpected and often tragic ways. This appendix provides a breakdown of Elliott's decisions and how they parallel real-life lessons about the human condition.

1. The First Wish: Wealth and Its Illusions

- **Choice Analysis**: Elliott's first wish for wealth, specifically to win the lottery, taps into a universal human desire: the pursuit of financial security and the belief that money can solve most problems. His decision to make this wish without considering its potential ramifications reflects the common tendency to view wealth as the ultimate solution to life's challenges.
- **Consequences**: While Elliott's wish is granted, the price is immediate and severe—he loses his job. This trade-off underscores a critical lesson: financial gain does not come without sacrifice. In real life, those who attain sudden wealth often find that it disrupts their existing structures, leading to challenges such as strained relationships, loss of purpose, and the burden of managing newfound assets.
- **Real-Life Reflection**: The "lottery curse" is a documented phenomenon where lottery winners face sudden financial, social, and personal turmoil. Elliott's loss of employment after becoming rich highlights the idea that wealth can isolate rather than liberate, showing that true satisfaction cannot be bought.

2. The Second Wish: Fame and the Loss of Privacy

- **Choice Analysis**: Driven by restlessness and the desire for meaning, Elliott wishes for fame as a world-renowned author. This wish symbolizes the human craving for recognition, admiration, and validation. Many people, whether artists, entrepreneurs, or influencers, pursue public acclaim, often without foreseeing the associated costs.
- **Consequences**: Elliott's rapid ascent to fame brings relentless media attention, obsessed fans, and a loss of personal privacy. The joy of recognition quickly sours as his home becomes besieged by paparazzi, and he receives threatening and invasive messages from fans. The story demonstrates how fame, while alluring, often traps individuals in a cycle of scrutiny, making them prisoners of their public personas.
- **Real-Life Reflection**: The stories of celebrities who struggle with their fame are countless. Public figures often find that the spotlight magnifies their vulnerabilities, turning what seemed like a dream into a source of stress and danger. Elliott's experience reflects the cautionary tale that fame without boundaries can strip away peace of mind and safety.

3. The Third Wish: The Return of Lost Companionship

- **Choice Analysis**: Elliott's final wish is born from a place of deep emotional need. Isolated by his wealth and fame, he yearns for the comfort and companionship of his deceased cat, Whiskers. This choice, unlike the others, is not driven by ambition or greed but by a desperate longing for solace and connection. It reflects the universal pain of loss and the instinct to reclaim what has been taken by time.
- **Consequences**: The resurrection of Whiskers is not the comforting reunion Elliott hoped for. Instead, it manifests as a sinister return, with the cat embodying the dark twist typical of the paw's power. This outcome teaches that some wishes, no matter how heartfelt, defy the natural order and carry unforeseen consequences. The familiar turned monstrous becomes a powerful metaphor for how tampering with fate often results in unintended chaos.
- **Real-Life Reflection**: People often struggle with accepting loss, whether it be the death of a loved one, a failed relationship, or past glory. The temptation to hold onto or recreate these experiences can lead to destructive behaviors or choices, such as clinging to the past or making impulsive decisions that backfire. Elliott's experience with Whiskers serves as a reminder that some voids cannot be filled without consequence and that true healing comes from acceptance, not defiance of natural laws.

Lessons in Greed, Ambition, and Boundaries

Elliott's story encapsulates the pitfalls of unchecked ambition. Each of his wishes was driven by a yearning that, while understandable, ultimately reflected a lack of foresight and a refusal to heed caution. The narrative highlights these key lessons:

- **Greed and Shortcuts**: The wish for sudden wealth and fame demonstrates the allure of shortcuts to success and prosperity. However, as Elliott's experience shows, these shortcuts can undermine long-term stability and lead to unexpected losses. The lesson here is that pursuing wealth and recognition without careful consideration of the ramifications can lead to personal and emotional ruin.
- **The Double-Edged Sword of Fame**: The story serves as a stark reminder that fame often comes at a steep price. Elliott's descent into paranoia and fear mirrors real-life accounts of individuals who found fame to be more of a burden than a blessing. It teaches that seeking validation from others is fraught with risks, and the personal cost of losing anonymity can be profound.
- **The Danger of Defying Nature**: The final wish, where Elliott attempts to bring Whiskers back, reinforces the idea that some desires cross into dangerous territory. The attempt to rewrite the laws of life and death comes with severe consequences, illustrating that accepting the limits of reality is often wiser than trying to alter them.

The Cautionary Framework of Folklore

Elliott's tale is rooted in the tradition of folklore that uses storytelling as a way to impart lessons about human nature. Like *The Monkey's Paw* and other classic stories such as *Faust* and *King Midas*, the narrative teaches that ambition, when pursued without moral or practical boundaries, leads to a fall. These stories serve as warnings, cautioning readers against letting desires cloud judgment and advocating for the balance between aspiration and humility.

Final Reflections

Elliott Barker's choices are both relatable and tragic, serving as a mirror to our own inclinations toward wanting more—more wealth, more acknowledgment, more happiness. But the caution embedded within *The Cursed Paw of Ambition* is that seeking fulfillment without understanding the true cost can twist even the purest desires into sources of anguish. It's a reminder that ambition is most powerful when paired with wisdom and that the pursuit of more should not come at the expense of what truly matters: peace, purpose, and acceptance.

The story leaves readers with a haunting question: *What would you wish for, knowing that the cost might be more than you're willing to pay?*

Journal Prompt: *What would you wish for, knowing that the cost might be more than you're willing to pay?*

Message from the Author:

I hope you enjoyed this book, I love astrology and knew there was not a book such as this out on the shelf. I love metaphysical items as well. Please check out my other books:

-Life of Government Benefits

-My life of Hell

-My life with Hydrocephalus

-Red Sky

-World Domination:Woman's rule

-World Domination:Woman's Rule 2: The War

-Life and Banishment of Apophis: book 1

-The Kidney Friendly Diet

-The Ultimate Hemp Cookbook

-Creating a Dispensary(legally)

-Cleanliness throughout life: the importance of showering from childhood to adulthood.

-Strong Roots: The Risks of Overcoddling children

-Hemp Horoscopes: Cosmic Insights and Earthly Healing

- Celestial Hemp Navigating the Zodiac: Through the Green Cosmos

-Astrological Hemp: Aligning The Stars with Earth's Ancient Herb

-The Astrological Guide to Hemp: Stars, Signs, and Sacred Leaves

-Green Growth: Innovative Marketing Strategies for your Hemp Products and Dispensary

-Cosmic Cannabis

-Astrological Munchies

-Henry The Hemp

-Zodiacal Roots: The Astrological Soul Of Hemp

- **Green Constellations: Intersection of Hemp and Zodiac**

-Hemp in The Houses: An astrological Adventure Through The Cannabis Galaxy
-Galactic Ganja Guide
Heavenly Hemp
Zodiac Leaves
Doctor Who Astrology
Cannastrology
Stellar Satvias and Cosmic Indicas
<u>Celestial Cannabis: A Zodiac Journey</u>
AstroHerbology: The Sky and The Soil: Volume 1
AstroHerbology:Celestial Cannabis:Volume 2
Cosmic Cannabis Cultivation
The Starry Guide to Herbal Harmony: Volume 1
The Starry Guide to Herbal Harmony: Cannabis Universe: Volume 2
Yugioh Astrology: Astrological Guide to Deck, Duels and more
Nightmare Mansion: Echoes of The Abyss
Nightmare Mansion 2: Legacy of Shadows
Nightmare Mansion 3: Shadows of the Forgotten
Nightmare Mansion 4: Echoes of the Damned
The Life and Banishment of Apophis: Book 2
Nightmare Mansion: Halls of Despair
<u>Healing with Herb: Cannabis and Hydrocephalus</u>
<u>Planetary Pot: Aligning with Astrological Herbs: Volume 1</u>
Fast Track to Freedom: 30 Days to Financial Independence Using AI, Assets, and Agile Hustles
<u>Cosmic Hemp Pathways</u>
How to Become Financially Free in 30 Days: 10,000 Paths to Prosperity
Zodiacal Herbage: Astrological Insights: Volume 1
Nightmare Mansion: Whispers in the Walls
The Daleks Invade Atlantis
Henry the hemp and Hydrocephalus

10X The Kidney Friendly Diet

Cannabis Universe: Adult coloring book

Hemp Astrology: The Healing Power of the Stars

Zodiacal Herbage: Astrological Insights: Cannabis Universe: Volume 2

<u>Planetary Pot: Aligning with Astrological Herbs: Cannabis Universes: Volume 2</u>

Doctor Who Meets the Replicators and SG-1: The Ultimate Battle for Survival

Nightmare Mansion: Curse of the Blood Moon

<u>The Celestial Stoner: A Guide to the Zodiac</u>

Cosmic Pleasures: Sex Toy Astrology for Every Sign

Hydrocephalus Astrology: Navigating the Stars and Healing Waters

Lapis and the Mischievous Chocolate Bar

Celestial Positions: Sexual Astrology for Every Sign

Apophis's Shadow Work Journal: : A Journey of Self-Discovery and Healing

Kinky Cosmos: Sexual Kink Astrology for Every Sign

Digital Cosmos: The Astrological Digimon Compendium

Stellar Seeds: The Cosmic Guide to Growing with Astrology

Apophis's Daily Gratitude Journal

Cat Astrology: Feline Mysteries of the Cosmos

The Cosmic Kama Sutra: An Astrological Guide to Sexual Positions

Unleash Your Potential: A Guided Journal Powered by AI Insights

Whispers of the Enchanted Grove

Cosmic Pleasures: An Astrological Guide to Sexual Kinks

369, 12 Manifestation Journal

Whisper of the nocturne journal(blank journal for writing or drawing)

The Boogey Book

Locked In Reflection: A Chastity Journey Through Locktober

Generating Wealth Quickly:

How to Generate $100,000 in 24 Hours

Star Magic: Harness the Power of the Universe

The Flatulence Chronicles: A Fart Journal for Self-Discovery

The Doctor and The Death Moth

Seize the Day: A Personal Seizure Tracking Journal

The Ultimate Boogeyman Safari: A Journey into the Boogie World and Beyond

Whispers of Samhain: 1,000 Spells of Love, Luck, and Lunar Magic: Samhain Spell Book

Apophis's guides:

Witch's Spellbook Crafting Guide for Halloween

Frost & Flame: The Enchanted Yule Grimoire of 1000 Winter Spells

The Ultimate Boogey Goo Guide & Spooky Activities for Halloween Fun

Harmony of the Scales: A Libra's Spellcraft for Balance and Beauty

The Enchanted Advent: 36 Days of Christmas Wonders

Nightmare Mansion: The Labyrinth of Screams

Harvest of Enchantment: 1,000 Spells of Gratitude, Love, and Fortune for Thanksgiving

The Boogey Chronicles: A Journal of Nightly Encounters and Shadowy Secrets

The 12 Days of Financial Freedom: A Step-by-Step Christmas Countdown to Transform Your Finances

Sigil of the Eternal Spiral Blank Journal

A Christmas Feast: Timeless Recipes for Every Meal

Holiday Stress-Free Solutions: A Survival Guide to Thriving During the Festive Season

Yu-Gi-Oh! Holiday Gifting Mastery: The Ultimate Guide for Fans and Newcomers Alike

Holiday Harmony: A Hydrocephalus Survival Guide for the Festive Season

Celestial Craft: The Witch's Almanac for 2025 – A Cosmic Guide to Manifestations, Moons, and Mystical Events

Doctor Who: The Toymaker's Winter Wonderland

Tulsa King Unveiled: A Thrilling Guide to Stallone's Mafia Masterpiece

Pendulum Craft: A Complete Guide to Crafting and Using Personalized Divination Tools

Nightmare Mansion: Santa's Eternal Eve

Starlight Noel: A Cosmic Journey through Christmas Mysteries

The Dark Architect: Unlocking the Blueprint of Existence

Surviving the Embrace: The Ultimate Guide to Encounters with The Hugging Molly

The Enchanted Codex: Secrets of the Craft for Witches, Wiccans, and Pagans

Harvest of Gratitude: A Complete Thanksgiving Guide

Yuletide Essentials: A Complete Guide to an Authentic and Magical Christmas

Celestial Smokes: A Cosmic Guide to Cigars and Astrology

Living in Balance: A Comprehensive Survival Guide to Thriving with Diabetes Insipidus

Cosmic Symbiosis: The Venom Zodiac Chronicles

If you want solar for your home go here: https://www.harborsolar.live/apophisenterprises/

Get Some Tarot cards: https://www.makeplayingcards.com/sell/apophis-occult-shop

Get some shirts: https://www.bonfire.com/store/apophis-shirt-emporium/

Instagrams:
@apophis_enterprises,
@apophisbookemporium,
@apophisscardshop
Twitter: @apophisenterpr1
Tiktok:@apophisenterprise
Youtube: @sg1fan23477, @FiresideRetreatKingdom
Hive: @sg1fan23477
CheeLee: @SG1fan23477
Podcast: Apophis Chat Zone: https://open.spotify.com/show/5zXbrCLEV2xzCp8ybrfHsk?si=fb4d4fdbdce44dec

Newsletter: https://apophiss-newsletter-27c897.beehiiv.com/